SUNDRE

SUNDRE

A Novel

CHRISTOPHER WILLARD

ESPLANADE
Books
THE FICTION SERIES AT VÉHICULE PRESS

Published with the generous assistance of The Canada Council for
the Arts and the Book Publishing Industry Development Program of
the Department of Canadian Heritage.

Esplanade Books editor: Andrew Steinmetz
Cover design: David Drummond
Set in Adobe Minion and Copperplate Gothic by Simon Garamond
Printed by Marquis Book Printing Inc.

LIBRARY AND ARCHIVES CANADA CATALOGUING IN PUBLICATION

Willard, Christopher, 1960-

Sundre : a novel / Christopher Willard.

ISBN 978-1-55065-253-6

I. Title.

PS3623.I4622 S86 2009   813'.6   C2009-900674-X

Published by Véhicule Press, Montréal, Québec, Canada
www.vehiculepress.com

Distribution in Canada by LitDistCo
www.litdistco.ca

Distribution in U.S. by Independent Publishers Group
www.ipgbook.com

Printed in Canada on 100% post-consumer recycled paper.

for Laurel

Locations of Indebtedness

Maya Assouad, Robert Coover, Simon Dardick, Dave Margoshes, Gord Moore, Kimberly Smee, Bryan Smith, Adam Sol, Andrew Steinmetz, Jean Winter, Leah Zelin, Calgary Public Library, Sundre and District Historical Society, University of Calgary Library.

The author would also like to thank the Alberta Foundation for the Arts for its generous support.

I didn't want to take a shot but I couldn't deny this woman.
You don't ask someone to go and shoot you.
You don't rush such decisions.
I took my time.
Rosedale Suspension Bridge.
I didn't need a plaque to tell me. I talked as I moved.
What a guy won't do for love.

— I just put a leg over the railing. I hoisted myself over, do you remember?

— You went far out there.

— True. That wasn't the easiest part.

— Swung onto the outside edge of that footbridge.

The whipped water of the Red Deer flew below me. Oh I made sure my foot was solid on the overhanging edge, alright.

— I can swim no problem. I won't be getting drowned.

— Even so.

I pulled my waist in close to the wood. It was a matter of getting my footing. Then I got the right grip and steadied my weight. Long way down to that tan water.

I clutched the camera with my free hand.

— Maybe you think it is more dangerous than it really is. Even so.

I found it hard to grip.

— I want to compose the picture and then I'll fairly propose.

— You won't get an answer today.

— Just don't make me suffer.

Sandra walked to the centre of that swinging bridge.

— See, I placed both feet on the beam.

— Avery...

I felt safer with my shoes tucked under the lip.

— Now I'm waiting.

— I'll marry you then. I'd marry you anyway, picture or not.

— You'll marry me no matter what.

I fumbled with the rangefinder, working the dial with my thumb until the film wouldn't advance any farther.

— Smile for the camera.

Steadily, steady, I aimed and glanced elsewhere.

— Remember how sweltering a day it was?
— Broken only by an oven wind.
— I sure as hell was a cocksure buck wasn't I?
— There was no hell in it.
— How easily I spun bluster into turf.

What I did without thought. What I did *with* thought. Things later I wouldn't have wished upon my sons to even think about doing.

— It all passed like the river, didn't it?
— You're content now?
— Contentedness is recognition.

Sandra kept that photograph in her bedroom, tucked into the dark frame that held her mirror.
The stillness of time settled silently upon those young faces. I measured time by dust.

— Film is time without comment, without justification or apology.
— Still.

Sometimes, when I looked at this picture closely, I could see.

I could see tiny stars of sweat forming above her eyebrows.
I could see an expectant radiance upon her cheeks.
I could see a thin glow of sky just above her lip.

Shoot me, I said.

Well, I didn't ask him that way.

Like that. Not like that.

That makes it sound so cut and dried, so calculated.

I didn't want it to sound that way.

I told him it would allow for a remembrance of particularity. Like the birds.

On frigid days the little feathereds snipped sunflower seeds; they seemed to take pleasure in the sun that eased across the land.

You're just crazy, he said.

— I'll marry you in a week, if you want, providing you can make the dress.

Dode was already more than a gleam.

Avery crooked a leg up over the handrail.

— Dangerous. Too dangerous just to get a shot.

— Don't get all up and over on this.

— I'm not looking to be widowed, from drowning even.

— It's called motherly worrying.

— When he or she comes I'll name it Damn Fool, after his father. What do you think about that?

I patted my relatively flat stomach.

— Call it what you want to call it, he answered. Others will probably call it many worse things. That won't be any business of mine.

I pinched the brim of my straw hat, the one decorated with a newly plucked rose, and I looked toward my man and I allowed the wind to clear my face of hair.

— I want to be remembered for who I was seen to be.

— Who were you seen to be?

— A woman with qualities, a courteous kindness for example.

He hooked his fingers around the railing and darned if he didn't lean out too, farther than I wished. And he snapped the camera with his free hand and then he climbed back onto the safety of the bridge.

— Oh I know this sounds terrible, all so presuming. Yet, I tried to bring qualities like that to those around me: you, our children, our dear friends.

— Or was it dear you, and our dear children, and our friends?

— Their photographs adorned our parlour and their faces adorn my dreams. Once they were touchable.

We elapse. We pass over and around and on and beyond. We move to whatever exists and we flit through dim reflections.

— Think of and remember the tang of salt on the tongue.

I sat on the porch, even in the bitterness of winter, and I watched the birds hover around the wooden feeder Avery had suspended from the eave.

Brown, dusty, claw-legged and shifting sparrows for the most part. They seemed continually nervous, hopping from bush to feeder, feeder to bush. When they cracked seeds I could see their shivers.

I could see their puffs of breath.
I could see frost in their bodies.
I could see ice in their souls.

A path, a picnic, a bridge. These are strong. Solid. The proposal was solid, but in a different way.

— I wish you hadn't worried, Avery.
— I did, about my failings.
— The insurance was paid in full.
— I want total clarity.
— Don't second guess. You can't sink a shining nail into a rusted past.

— Events are like spots of light. Like what happened to that Gilmore boy.

— And the others. A naturalness at least punctuates the unnaturalness of the accident. It's the suffering that gets to me the most.

— You are made more human by the amount you ease suffering.

— I suffered too.

— We all did.

Nothing soothing in suffering. No good reason for it, and even when there's a reason it's usually a crumb poor one. I read the Good Book, not cover to cover, not start to finish or enough to quote, but enough. Not a reluctant word in those pages about relieving suffering.

I find more reassurance in the seasons: in a time when roots thrust up sap and a field is opened; a time when tears squirt from beneath stones; a time when a row ripens to stiff, husky stalks; a time when trees ache and you can't set a pike.

— What about summer?

— Think of hot black-treaded tires one could slap a hand upon.

— And what about Dode?

— Lanky boy. More ideas than a tree full of crows. You think I don't remember?

I remember icicles reflecting the fields. On their tips, droplets reflecting the house. And below, puddles reflecting the sky.

I remember much.

I remember Dode as he once stood straddling the puddle, head tilted toward the chinook arch as he caught the dripping water in his mouth.

Snowflakes as broad as my fingernail fell the morning Dode arrived. I remember thinking how like children the flakes were. Formed from a single drop, each grew into its own carefully crafted lattice of nature-tattered pattern. How symmetrical. How unique.

— His birth was a moment of tense muscles and beaming pride.

— You didn't worry then? Never?

— You must think it's a woman's right to worry. I didn't worry.

— You worried when the tractor rolled sideways onto Brandon Gilmore. A stocky boy killed by a small hill. And there were those other boys at the junction.

— You can see why I worried.

— It's wrong of me to revisit everything. It makes it sound like I don't understand.

— And I didn't worry all the time.

— I worried too. I just didn't say so because, like you, I wasn't interested in creating a fuss.

When Eve was tempted to the apple there was no worry. She knew she would have tasted it anyway. The unknown is framed as good or evil but what it offers most is seduction and beauty. Methods are only moments upon a path. What remains is what we dwell upon and we dwell within what remains.

— That's what women are. That's what men are.

—And Dode?

— I remember Dode's thoughtfulness. And I remember his forgetfulness. And, I remember his blessedness.

These are the things I remember.

— Anything else?

To remember is to shift.
To remember is to separate and stand upon a pedestal.

— I remember a head full of thick wheaty hair and milky eyes like February clouds.

My father first touched this land. From that larch silhouetting the yellow sky all the way to that stone foundation. His brother lived in a house there. Given and given back when he scuffed an exit to Winnipeg with his wife and belongings.

Suddenly my father owned one front door too many. Oh the land was alright, but he was keen to sell the structure. He posted an ad and some city fella ate the dust all the way up here and then stood by his car with a surveying eye.

This house, shed, barn. Land as far as I can see, my father said.

Not a bad deal, said the man.

Damn fashionable deal, if you ask me, my father said.

The man stretched a grin and peered toward territory running back to the mountains. Pennies on the dollar.

Nobody had built on that side of Sundre. We bordered sacred land, Stoney Nakoda land. But it's all sacred land to me.

I may need a few days to see the deed clear, the man said.

Now or never.

The man chose now.

He returned a few days later madder than H-E double hockey sticks.

Only an acre on this deed. You cheated me half way up a cow's tail, that's what you did.

I said as plain truth, land as far as I can see, it's just I don't see very good.

The story isn't true of course. Place burned down not long after he moved away. That's the foundation over by the bushes.

My father, myself, my two sons, we have all sifted this soil. Our lineage is dug and tilled.

I've scratched the surface of my plot with my foot and my fingers and nearly every tool I've owned. In return those few inches of dirt provided me the sole reason to stay.

And Sandra. Sweet clover is what she liked best.

I couldn't have asked for a better companion. Contented, patient, a good mother and wife, delicate of character, unfaltering in her duty as a woman. We made it a rule never to swaddle a begrudging thought with a pillow. I think about that advice. I don't know where I got it, certainly not from my parents who fought 'till noon of night and in whose kitchen a towel was always being slapped against one wall or cupboard.

— Some things just blow around and people pick them up.

— There's no doubt you were the flower of my entire existence. Never did I find a more constant perennial.

Into the same book she used to record our genealogy, she pressed flowers: sweet clover, monkey flowers. She tucked rein orchids between pages inked with dates of those born and dates of those married and dates of those long deceased.

— Are they only memories?

— They have changed just as the ocean turns to rain and rain turns to snow and snow turns to water.

From here the land stretches like pulled dough, with sloping meadows and wavy earthen foothills. This is a country of tawny sienna and dusty umber.

— You made it green.

— For a moment.

The only greens remaining are temperate greens, olive, a frail Hooker's green, a swart punctuation on a land that will always and eventually return to its burnt origin.

I dug my hands into this sod. I sifted dirt from the flower bed with fingers of many ages. That's a knowledge better than any book.

Outsiders define us Albertans a brash people who look back on busted futures and see encouragement in the earth's arid skin. We speak our minds, yes. Taking charge becomes a habit. You have to out here, otherwise the elements will harness your spirit.

When I first looked across these foothills, I swelled up with a promise of growth and of prosperity, of feed and food, of plant and plant-eaters.

Now I gaze over oceanic fields that sway and silently nudge the ankles of the Rockies. Never did a *No Trespassing* sign deface our land. Our fences had stiles. We maintained a congeniality of borders, a tangible handshake of neighbourliness.

— It kept us busy though, didn't it?

— What a section of my life was spent moving the land or moving that which was grown from the land.

What time I spent picking up things: kittens, children, colanders, columbine.

And the rest of the time, I ran needles through heels of wool socks; I kneaded until my shoulders and arms were strong, ox sinew.

— Too busy to complain, my mother used to say.

On early spring evenings I wrapped against the chill and sat on the porch and watched bluebirds dart from one to another of the boxes we nailed to fence posts. One bird blue and orange one bird blue and blue. They cocked ever vigilant heads toward grass cow-licked by the wind. Cotton shifted overhead: bear-shift-hare-shift and on past dark eaves. A hollow clutch-grind wafted from beyond the rise in the road. From the east floated the wavering resonance of a working tractor. On the railing a fly presented its glory of late day iridescence.

Laughable really. Picking through this jar of colourful glass marbles. Once I clutched at them and held them in a tight private fist.

— You can't hold forever.
— I am woman foremost. I carry and coddle.

Allow me this.

— I recall the pungent wooly fragrance of the sweet clover and I feel that we are closer now than we were before.
— Closer to what?

Still, I held tight.
Later, in the solitude of my room, I opened my hand and found only my palm.

— You should learn how to do this.

Dusty gnawed at his fingernail.

— Didn't I say she'd be due before the geese quit their migration? Important to get it into your head and hands.

Sandra had the midwife on alert. She too was ready to bring into the world a living thing.

— We have enough to do out here in the barn.

Dusty nodded.

— Third foal since you were born. All yours this time. Name it what you wish. See how the udder's dropped? That's milk dripping from her teats. Sign she'll be foaling any time now.

I collected a little milk in a jar and held it to the window. It was thick, syrupy, the colour of a light honey.

Dusty ran his hand across the horse's neck.

— Just because they invented cars doesn't mean we don't love you.

He told her lots of things to calm her.

— You're of the land.

He told her the details about his last trip to the Calgary Stampede because he'd run out of words and you can only say good horse and nice horse so many times before it all starts to sound like a frayed fan belt.

I sat on one of the kitchen chairs I'd hauled out and I zipped my coat and I lit a cigarette. The smoke twisted through the sun shafts like a blue plant growing up toward the rafters. The mare pawed at her straw bedding.

I sent Dusty for some blankets and an old sheet.

I patted the mare's thigh. She was a pretty one. Fourteen and a half hands high. Spots across her shoulder looked like blown snow. Another patch on her rump looked like a flying dove. Sandra agreed with me on that. The horse turned her head as though respecting the strength of my hand. Trust is bedrock.

34

— Here's the sheet.

— How's your ma doing in there?

— She told me to get the sheet and get out.

— That means she's doing fine.

I told him to tear it into strips.

Dusty tore the sheet and as he handed me each strand I wrapped it around the mare's tail, tying off the last one with a small knot.

We waited.

Dusty whittled away most of a poplar stick with his toad stabber and I smoked a number of slow cigarettes.

After a while the mare lay upon the straw with her chest bulging and flattening. At other times her whole frame shuddered and contracted.

— Shouldn't we call the vet or something?

— This is what horses do. Horses have horses. Been having horses ever since they ran. You know about feral horses.

— Well, yeah.

— Nature knows what it needs. You think she doesn't know what's happening?

We waited until the horse eventually became restless and we let her be until the front feet of the foal appeared, one sticking out farther than the other, her nose nestled between them.

The mare heaved her head in order to look and then flopped against the wooden slat.

Once free, the foal lay beyond its mother. Its eyes were two blue ponds in a white winter.

We towelled its hair and I removed the jackknife from my pants pocket and cut about a foot length of string. Then I dipped the blade into a seven percent iodine that I kept in a jar for just this purpose.

— Prevents infection.

I handed the knife to Dusty and I twisted the string around the umbilical cord.

35

— Some would call this a ghost horse.

— I could call it that.

— Right here.

Dusty ran the knife through the umbilical cord.

— Little Ghost.

He handed me back my knife and I wiped it on the towel while the foal sort of crawled toward its mother as though the mare was all it knew in life.

Eventually the mother hoisted herself around and began to lick the mucus from her foal's muzzle.

— Listen.

Dusty raised his chin.

From the house we heard Sandra's call.

Dusty looked away from my gaze.

— Nothing we can do. Better we waste some time.

Dusty bottle fed the foal some of the colostrum and then we grabbed it by the haunches and helped it to stand. It eventually found its mother and nuzzled around as if to suckle. Not that it mattered.

— She's beautiful isn't she.

— A foal stolen from an angel's chariot.

— Little Ghost.

— Pure cloud. You get a white one only once in a blue moon.

Neither brings remedy.

Breath. Breath. Foal breath and smoky breath. I've warmed air and I've exhaled with force. In a chill barn on a chill day I've puffed air that was gone before I hardly recognized it.

— Sometimes I wonder whether in this world something can be good without something being terrible. My tongue snags like barbed wire. You're the poet.

— You said it well enough.

— Even that brief, beautiful moment we call life ends terribly.

— Don't use that word. Nothing terrible in endings.

— Would a baby choose to live, knowing the terrible future it would continually strive towards?

I have strong dirty hands, one blackened nail.

These are the fingers and hands that forged things. These fingers are solid. This hand is solid.

This hand was solid.

From inside the house we heard a new voice, a high bawling holler. Dusty ran from the barn, or I thought he did. And as soon as he left I slapped that mare alright, as hard as I could, a cuff to the side of her snout. Damn devil seed. I slapped her so hard my hand turned purple.

— Papa?

Dusty had waited in the fine light.

—Why hit her? She's a good horse. She'll be a good mother.

Think about ants. Think about locusts and worms. Think about the bug-bloody fender following a drive back from E-town. Think about what you don't want to think about.

I learned it's all one big farm with God at the top. He has his fenced-in angels, he pens a livestock of souls.

And I learned he puts creatures on earth for humans, plants for animals, and so on down. We're all useful for something. Even a charred bone can be used to draw an unbroken circle.

First time I swaddled Sheryn-Lee I wrapped her in a fuzzy yellow blanket and held her up to face the land and she gurgled to tell me there was more than flat.

Dusty rocketed into the bedroom to disclose the foal amid shushes, blushes.

— I have a new horse. I named her Little Ghost. And I'll take really good care of her and there will be a whole beam of ribbons above her stall.

I carefully handed the baby back to Sandra.

— Now we let them be.

The next day I strode across the stiff grass to check on the foal and found the stall empty. Nearby on the floor lay an old door and a curled blanket. Through the hazy pane I could see the blurry impression of Dusty clinging to the top of the wooden fence as he watched the foal romp near its mother.

The corners of the window's muntin bars were filigreed with spun web, catchalls of grasses, flies, moths.

Look and then answer me in the same line.

The spiders were now hollow shells, like their prey, like the strands of alfalfa, like the carcasses of moths.

I know, I dwell on endings.

I dwell on endings even though I dislike endings. They linger and loiter and they run haywire around our insides. Eventually they sober us up.

Dusty yelled at the horses and I was suddenly aware of a rank, musty smell. I considered three, mare, foal, son. Eventually I shuffled out of the barn and into the field.

— She's acting funny.

Instead of suckling, the foal bumped its nose into its mother. Then finding no comfort, the little thing whinnied and threw itself onto the ground where it rolled back and forth. The top of her tail was raw and red where she'd been nipping at herself.

— How long you seen this?

— Mostly all morning. But she was acting restless last night too, that's why I let them out.

— I suspect you should get your brother.

Dusty hopped down off the fence and ran. I followed and I closed my eyes and let the wind gust across my cheek.

Dode came onto the porch and stretched.

— Wha' ya want? I got to work later today.

He had a part-time job down at Bergen's convenience and gas.

— You and your brother take and put a rope on the foal and lead it out to the edge of the pasture, back by the bales, I'll be there momentarily.

I went upstairs to the bedroom where Sandra was nursing the baby. I brushed my hand across my wife's forehead. Then I took my .22 from out of the closet and a box of bullets off the top shelf.

— I don't like seeing a gun in the same room as a baby.

— Foal's sick.

She looked toward the gun then at me.

— Charlie Olstad had one a few years ago. Lethal white. A

paint has its foal and the breeding causes its intestines to tie up. Can't eat, and even if it does it ends up bloating and dying in a week.

— Your son loves that horse I think.

I put the bullets in my jacket pocket and went to the barn where I fetched the pick and a shovel before slowly walking across the field.

The boys were trying to calm the foal which now was thrashing from side to side against the ground and when Dusty saw me he jumped away from the animal.

— Papa, No.

— She got a sickness inside, Dusty. She's suffering.

— We can just call the vet.

— Not for this one. She can't eat.

— I saw her suckle today.

— Can't digest. Its guts are all wound up in knots.

Dusty squinched his eyes shut.

— Dode you hold it down by putting your knee on its neck.

Dode did what I told him and I took the rope and tied the foal's back legs together. Then I tied the front legs. It was a makeshift hobble to settle it.

Dusty dropped beside the foal and wrapped its arms around the head of the poor animal.

— You'll have to shoot me too because I won't let you hurt Little Ghost.

There are times when saying nothing says more than a cart of explaining. And when I felt I had said nothing long enough I took the box of bullets out of my coat pocket and I opened the cardboard flap and I took out two bullets and slid them into the gun.

— She'll just suffer and it will get worse and then what? Think about it. It will be worse if she suffers.

Dusty stayed.

— Dode, give me a hand here.

Dode reached for Dusty's arm.

— No, I can handle Dusty. Take the gun and keep it pointed away from us.

I handed the gun to Dode.

— This is my pony. I should say.

I moved with the intention of yanking Dusty away, but he sprung back on his own.

— Stay calm. I don't want anyone getting hurt because of some foolishness.

The wind flapped at Dusty's open jacket and I took the rifle and held it out for my youngest.

· — You're going to help run this farm some day. And you're going to have to recognize it's always a cycle. Things get born things die.

That was my learning. Even so it sounded like an unfinished sentence.

Dusty grabbed the gun and immediately set it on the ground between us. He wiped at his eyes with a grubby hand and he smeared dark, life-giving Alberta dirt across his wet face. I slid my handkerchief from my back pocket and handed it to him and we waited while he wiped his face. Overhead flew honking vees of geese like trails of dark smoke.

— Ok son.

Dusty folded the handkerchief and threw it down beside the rifle. He looked past me with eyes that were glassy and glossy.

— It's sick, Dode finally said.

The wind picked up. For some reason I recalled how the wind once blew over a cow and we joked that we bred cows for beef not balance.

— Let's get this done and we'll go in and see if we can find some bacon and some eggs to fry up. Surprise your ma.

Dusty picked up the .22 by the barrel.

— Jeez Louise, said Dode.

— You know better than to handle a gun that way.

Dusty tipped the gun and placed one hand on the mahogany stock and another on the trigger guard.

— I'm sorry Little Ghost. I'm not doing this. They are making me do this.

He pumped the handle and moved the cocked gun toward the animal who strained against the rope and twisted its neck as though trying to nudge the weapon away.

— Not her chest. If you have to do it, you want it merciful.

Dusty pointed the gun in the direction of the foal but he kept swinging it past her head.

— Aim the damn thing or you'll just wound it, Dode said.

Dusty continued to shake, not just in his hands but in his arms and his legs. I was just about to reach in and take the gun when he fired into the dirt.

The shot scared the bejeezus out of me and it echoed across the prairie. A small smattering of dirt and some dust flew up but otherwise nothing moved until the sound died away. Even the foal relaxed, maybe from being tied up, maybe from some sixth sense.

Dusty pumped the gun again and sighted the barrel toward the lead coloured mountains and fired.

— Stop that recklessness.

I reached across his arm and took the rifle.

— Dode.

Dusty backed away and started running toward home. We watched him climb over the fence and only then did I double-check the gun was empty. I picked up my handkerchief and we untied the foal and I patted Dode on the shoulder and I breathed.

I thought, a man can take a broad breath out here.

Sometimes ending suffering means creating suffering. No learning reconciles that, no book teaches you how to balance those kinds of bales. You just pick them up and throw them on the wagon, you move to the next, you stack them high, you wipe the skin of your raw arm across your forehead, you carry your load.

The wind now brought the rain. I pulled my coat tight to my chest and I considered how that which is born brings joy yet reigns with sadness.

— Name her what you wish.

To Avery, having a baby is like yeaning. It's not at all the
same but I know what he means. That's how soft newborns
are.

Once my dresses flowed, flapped with the wind. Three times
the folds pressed against a belly ripe with the future. Dode,
Dusty, later Sheryn-Lee. Can't say my mother's *What a Young
Wife Ought to Know* was much use.

A newborn is a centre, a pinpointing exactitude, a locus
between vault of sky and plane of earth. A newborn modifies
air in commanding ways.

I named her Sheryn-Lee after my own mother.

She, Sheryn-Lee, was marked. A flush flowered her neck
like a dip of rose.

I met Avery at the April Fools' dance. He hung near the coffee urn. I found him handsome: flaxen face, freckled, fescue hair more unruly than unkempt. He probably figured I was ordinary in looks. Out here they'd say I didn't pretty much. I don't know that it mattered to him. Glamour is not a word yoked to prairie life. But, the future of a seventeen-year-old girl is one of fleeting dreams and pinching desire. I was bent on obtaining a teaching certificate so I might encourage a classroom of scribbling hands.

Nearly all of Sundre was out that day. They hoisted the young, wheeled the bedridden. A moment of summer tranquility, an official holiday between first planting and harvesting. The girls had made little sandwiches with cellophane between the meat, they'd dipped pickled onions into chocolate.

My robin's breast dress sure stood out.

I wore white socks. I danced to the Métis fiddles right up until 11:30 when Robbie Burkholder yelled into the microphone, Time to start the bidding!

I cradled my contribution to the midnight lunch, a picnic basket with its handle wrapped in orange ribbon to match my dress. I pushed the basket onto the stage and I was blind enough not to see some of the guys nudging Avery. Dang fool, he bid the thing up to one Canadian cartwheel and thirty-five cents. He cantered to the stage to claim his prize and he handed a dollar and a half to Robbie saying any girl who had thought of such a pretty ribbon must be worth an even number.

— Congratulations Mr. Avery, you won my lunch.

Can you ask for a more stupid statement than that?

He slid the handles over his arm and hauled a couple of folding wooden chairs outside. He placed them away from the light of the porch.

— Oh those no-see-ums.

— This is a darn good sandwich. You sure you don't want one?

— I tried the chicken when I made them this afternoon.

I bit my cheek in embarrassment. I should have followed my mother's advice never to pass up a good chance to shut up.

— You must think I'm stupid.

— How so?

— For using leftover chicken.

— You just go on making leftover chicken as good as this and I'll come by for lunch every night.

Such is the nonsense we talked that evening. Even so, my heart was hitched. Never did it waver, not even for an instant.

I never did make it back to school. I spent time improving my mind by reading poetry. I read it to the children too.

Sheryn-Lee was my last. A prairie wildflower. When my contractions got tight and regular I took the handmade quilts off the bed and had Avery call the midwife. I knew.

— They built the new hospital so people might use it.
— There's something in home comfort.

Nonetheless he called. Early on I walked, although that might be the incorrect word, hobbled with much help would be more accurate, and I sat on the swing. Something about the motion helped me deal with the cramps. Later I found the bed more cooperative.

Throughout my pregnancy my feet had been cold and that was supposed to signal a boy.

I turned my head. The eastern sky seemed small. I could see the land; the colours revealed the month. My breathing was paced, fluid. My breathing became the seasons of my early childhood in St. Thomas.

When another contraction came I held the pain close to my chest until it passed. I kicked aside sheets. Nothing much to be worried with.

My pains came on like surging storms and I sweated and I tossed. Just as quickly they released and I sipped water and I lay my wet cheek against the pillow and I dreamed.

The patterned wallpaper.

Stems flowed from mossy springs, the greens of the supple season.

The print on the wall, fields raged with crickets and bushes carpeted the land.

The glow of the midwife.

The tasselled lampshade, oranges and rusts raced across acre backswaths.

Here.

Out here, the land whispers the seasons. The most dramatic change is but a skiff of snow blowing across hard furrows.

The clouds are the signs.

Winter clouds are arced sheets originating from the arch of the snow eater, the chinook, a sky half-blue to the mountains, a bisection that in an entire day may move only across the peak of the house.

The warmer months arrive with the wind blowing from four corners. Spring bluster cuts stringy, slanting clouds. The the hot air jacks up clouds that tower high into the wispy atmosphere and the sky greys and bulbous clouds hang down like breasts.

Summer breezes scale the Rockies and push beyond their tops where flat, curving clouds, lenses, limp berets, hover over the tallest peaks.

The autumn clouds race toward colder nights. Their tops whip up like ocean curls, bleached ringlets, Greek waves.

Sheryn-Lee was a constantly tossing coral-hued lamb, agitated, yawning, bawling, thrusting legs and arms. She tried to grasp every compass point.

She lived before she was born. I knew that, if I knew anything. I don't require their theories. Her miniature heart ticked to the thump of my own. She moved in my skin, turned even. It's said that successive births are easier than the first. Mine was infinitely more painful. Perhaps because I'd waited nearly seven years to have my third.

So much for the wives' tales. Perhaps my feet were cold because Sheryn-Lee's feet were hot with the desire to travel. At nine months she walked from the sofa to the piano bench. By the time my tiny girl reached nine years she'd walked every fence edge. Once she nearly wore out a pair of shoes walking halfway to Olds.

There was originality in her birth in the way that perfect originality is found in the usual if only you take the time to look.

She suckled and then relaxed upon my chest. She blinked her transparent eyes and scanned the room. She curled and uncurled her fine-like-a-button fingers, crinkled, waxy. She clenched her hands as tightly as walnuts. She held the sunlight and the darkness with those tiny hands.

This little girl was my fear. She came into this room as though alone and when she rested against me I was mindful of my neediness. Our aloneness became a communal action.

I propped up Sheryn-Lee.
I was the stem and she the flower.
We sat on the porch. I held her wrist and pointed her finger
at the clouds.
Hill and breeze modified the tender ice crystals into puffs
and styles. It shaped and altered.

— There's a bunny. A snake over there.

I also saw an ogre from whose lopped head flowed cirrus
streams of frosty blood before it turned into a dancing calf.

— There's a calf. See how it dances!

Sheryn-Lee made the four-legged bench for 4-H, she wore
the blue and white tie and earned the Girl Guide badges in
cooking and homemaking; semaphore interested her more.
She sent signals. The mountains taunted her.
She'd prove the earth was bigger than her gaze.

When I was a little girl my hair was a dull blonde, the colour of memory. I stood in a musty one-room class with my finger against a globe and I traced a line that slid over seas and bumped over ranges. I landed on the Aral. The other side of the earth. Between us, people, continents, whole oceans, a globule of humanity and feeling, of blueness and white, of verdant oxygenated life. That little globe was more than primordial but less than utopia.

— Still, enough. Enough and more than enough.

We, like my Sheryn-Lee, thrust and clutch. Let our small hands shadow the strands of barrel rays that cut evening clouds. Let us flick dusty grains borne by summer's whispers. Let us skid our heels against the earth's mantel.

When the day was clear, I believed Sheryn-Lee might stand on a field of mud and look down the mouse holes, past the gopher holes, below the crust, through the fire, and again past the layers to the other side.

In high school she found her interior voice. She fashioned the horses in watercolour and she painted the wet skies by dipping her brush into a jar of tenderness. She borrowed a library book on a painter named Andrew Wyeth in whose work I recognized the haggard shimmer of dormant hoarfrost, glossed grasses, and the white slide of clean lit snow. Somehow he smacked the landscape onto paper.

We tried copying one or two of his paintings. Sheryn-Lee did alright; she captured a little joy with her strokes. My attempts turned glistening paper to pale distractions.

Sheryn-Lee continued.

I stopped and went to the window and looked across the fields and mounds and prairie lumps of burning purple, shifted ochre, poisoned yellows. I had subdued them beneath groggy

55

washes. To my left, complete views of a heliotrope and bee-eater blue, to the right crests of acrid ringing orange, shifts to satinwood, shafts of nutria.

Preposterous, really, that anyone could think they might lock this thrill with pigment. No amount of colour or gum arabic, no finesse of brush or wash could encase such visual lingerings. Ludicrous as trying to preserve a reflection.

Sometimes I remember the timbre of a voice.

Their voices, three of them.

Dode was the oldest, pragmatic, true. His voice was so much like his father's that I couldn't tell them apart without seeing. Dode wanted to plant, to settle, to grow. He stayed because he wanted to. He learned guitar. Sometimes he accompanied me on the piano. He played bluegrass, *I got a pig at home in a pen, corn to feed 'im on. All I need is a pretty little girl to feed 'im when I'm gone,* but he preferred his own music.

Then Dusty. Cleaved from my own image, same pale arms and darker circles under his eyes, a boy who'd burn more than tan. He was klutzy in a way, attacking the world with blunt vigour, mucking up half of what he touched, laughing off the mistakes.

Dusty spent hours collecting pictures of cars.

I'll go to the Institute, study mechanics, he said. Maybe open up a repair shop. Fix broken things. Make them new again.

While Dode imagined footstep following footstep, Dusty flew dreams like kites.

By the time Dusty gained on eleven years a new flag hung from our pole, eleven points. Designed by an Albertan. Avery flew it not out of patriotic attitude, his alliances lay within a close proximity, no, I think he flew it as a signal of our personal solidarity. He recognized just who we were and where we were. Exactly what that red leaf had to do with anything out here is beyond me. Look. Larches are yellow, firs prove green's durability. If there's a maple it's the bastard maple. Red is a colour from the other side of Winnipeg. From the land where I grew up, of the east, of sunrises, of the past.

We spent evenings in the kitchen; tiny Sheryn-Lee pointed out the queens until she squirmed too much. We played 500 mainly, using a regular deck if there were the four of us. When company came, I'd get from the top desk drawer the patterned BIJOU cards with the eleven and twelve spots. Dode had a good head for counting and saving up his trumps, knowing when to play Misère and when to dump. Me, well I never figured out counting for my life.

On Sheryn-Lee's eighteenth birthday her eyes suddenly turned a cooler hazel and they focused across the prairies toward Toronto. She took my mother's trunk and a portfolio.

Wind, and wind. *O Western wind, when wilt thou blow.* The wind here is ceaseless. On August days the furry wind is seen flying over fields, licking my arm, shoving my hair, forcing cotton tight around my legs. Toward the west anvil clouds rise like steam from a teakettle. The wind turns leaves. The cattle kneel against it. Trees call out with sweeping hisses, birds dissect the air with bent and pointed wings. The bull atop the barn turns east, then north. The fields flash bright sunflower yellow, a last protest below the dark steel of the approaching rain.

The smell of damp, of dirt. White lace curtains play out of the open upstairs windows. The house needs painting, soon but not today. A smoky gauze slants across the sky, pencil scratchings. A nervous magpie lets out a nasal *mag mag mag* from the blue spruce. Thunder crawls over the ground and clears out thoughts. The magpie wildly whirls away.

Sheryn-Lee left her spit upon this land. The word *town* became for her a curse, a wound.

My daughter moved far from this boundless expanse. She refused all but paved streets and timetables. She learned how to draw and paint. She learned how to be an artist. And how to be. But I didn't believe it.

58

Art cannot be taught. Life cannot be taught.

Reason is the filigree of emotion.

Sheryn-Lee believes the future includes the sunny, the laughing, the caress, the fervid.

My future enclosed and was enclosing. I was afraid of being alone. Sometimes my emotion was a rock howling in a quarry.

Long ago I sat, propped on pillows, with Sheryn-Lee sleeping beside me. I had the radio on and the gentle music played against to the occasional static of lightning I couldn't yet see. Sheryn-Lee's tiny head was cushioned by two pillows and she breathed in a rhythm all her own. A small bubble of spittle had formed on her delicate lips. Even then, as peaceful as it all was, even basking in a feeling best described as celebration, I knew that one day she would cross boundaries without regard or so much as a backward glance.

The child of the womb bawls forth joyfulness and sings forth misfortune.

I flew once in my life. Remember? With Harold "Bucky" Waindiff down there at the Calgary Stampede. He was a man who preferred beer and tomato juice, a Calgary Red-Eye we called it. Fifteen dollars. That's what that bastard charged to take me up in his glued together grasshopper. How he ever kept the thing running, I don't know. I joked with him and told him you don't slap the name *Nightingale* on something that's twenty shades of grey and all patched up with rubber cement and the bottoms of tin cans.

— Maybe they made things with a different sensibility back then.
— They didn't make them to last any more than they do now.
— I didn't like it then, I don't like it now. You don't squat with your spurs on.
— You're the one who nearly jumped off the bridge.
— Things were different.
— Things are different.

Maybe it was because of Sandra's prodding or maybe because I'd known Bucky at least as many years as he was charging dollars. Maybe it just got into me to lift my feet.
— You try any of those loops or wing waves and I'll knock your head into the next province.
He promised, slow and easy.
— Not too slow either. I don't want this junk bucket to be my coffin.
He strapped me sitting and then ran the jumper down the grass on the north side of the grounds. That thing smoked and roared and we bounced and bounced higher and that chuck-race oval quickly became a loop of dry rope and the coloured fields fell to square patches of quilting.

I knew that somewhere below me was my own chunk of land and I tried to pick it out but was unable to locate even the town.

Bucky gunned the engine toward the newer city buildings and I could see the tall one with the grass on top. He then turned sharply and the engine whined like a mule as he dipped directly over the stampede corrals. You should have seen some of those old horses. They cowered right down on the ground, scared out of their baggy skins probably thinking a gigantic horsefly was bearing upon their backs. When the plane landed I was jounced nearly out of my skull and I told Bucky that Rocky Rockabar would have had a smoother ride on the back of Widowmaker.

— Right then I vowed out loud that I would never, never get into a plane again. And I didn't, did I?

Sandra said she wouldn't mind flying, all the way to Hawaii even. I offered her right there to go up with Bucky and she could wave her arms while he flew the dang thing as far as he might over the Pacific Ocean and I said I'd come out with a boat to pick them up after they sent up the flares. She said she'd take me up on the offer too, but had decided against it, not because she was afraid but because of Bucky's rate. Bucky said he'd give us the next ride, half price. I snuffed at that one and I told him that men were meant to travel with soles flat to the earth.

I kept a .22 rifle and a shotgun with the provincial permit to use them both. A .22's velocity is faster, so it has more hitting power. But at close range the shotgun is a powerful weapon when loaded, especially when loaded with the double-aught. Then again, the rifle has a better range and accuracy, if that happens to be important.

She was just going off. She was most likely upset, looking through the picture window, thinking of all those birds she liked to watch, and knowing that I was heading out to hunt.

Partridge flew plentiful in those days. Over time the city spread chased them farther into the backcountry.

I pulled on my wet-boots and hiked the road and shot what I saw and after a while I figured I'd shot so many it felt a little short of murder. But then those partridges weren't the brightest birds, all but asking me to pick them off.

You fire a gun out there, no matter where really, and it makes an all out ear shattering noise. Half the province can probably hear the retort. I'm sure partridges can hear too, but the gun would bang and one partridge would drop and the others would just go on sitting there. That's why I call them stupid.

A sharp-tailed grouse walked in front of my sights once. I'd come upon a covey that was chattering and coo cooing. What good their brown backs and camouflage white spots did I don't know because their eyes were defined by fire orange rings that could be picked up from close to a hundred yards. They were much wilier. Wherever a group settled, one or two would post themselves as lookouts, just watching while the others ate. If I ever got close enough to be lucky with the trigger pull, the rest would scatter every which way.

I can't think the number of hares that were pointed at by these two guns, both in my time and in my father's time. He called it hunting jumper steak. I ended the life of most of the ones I pointed at. A couple of times, as a boy, I shot one badly, in the front leg maybe, and the thing started bawling and flopping on its twisted mess of hair and shining flesh, dragging itself through the dust and the grass. My father yelled at me.

— Damn poor aiming. You got to finish it off.

They were out of their misery soon enough.

Sandra never liked me telling those sorts of stories even when I tried to explain it was all part of the cycle.

— Not up to you to control such things.

Nature tells us one thing as truth: if we can't control our end, another will.

It's better this way, you said.

As a woman I followed you for most of my life, I answered. How shall I follow you into the future?

I know. My phrasing is skewed. I know that you cannot be and I cannot be and yet we talk as though we are right here. But still we are.

Somehow.

In some way.

Beyond.

After.

Ongoing.

Once I might have said, blessed be the creatures of the sky and earth for they know not what they do. I'm not so sure I can say that now.

What will not speak is often the best lecturer. What will not answer is often the best listener.

Try telling that to a seventeen-year-old roaring down Highway 7 cranked up on life with an open shirt and an open window, *Aquarius* leaping from the radio across tanned knuckles.

Avery was the sensible one, deliberate, convulsing in ramifications, plotting finishes, describing methodologies, fashioning *perhaps* into *definition*.

I preferred the sparrows.

In the spring of 1962 Jimmy Gilliam came to the door to let me know they'd started up a mail service. It snowed that day more than it had snowed all season and I looked at his pot tracks from car to steps and he told me he'd be doing the rounds three times a week if I ever wanted to send something without going in to town.

I mailed a letter, just to see if it worked more than to say anything.

Dusty shuffled to the counter where I was scraping. Sheryn-Lee was scribbling at the kitchen table with a crayon the same colour as the carrots.

— See my room?

— We wondered who was banging up a storm.

Dusty had brought home a bullet-riddled stop sign. I knew what he was doing.

— It will make a cool room decoration.

He was sixteen then. Two years younger than my eldest son.

— What'll your brother say?

— My side of the room.

We bear the children. We raise them. We plant and mill and knead. Grain becomes bread, it rises, browns.

I never asked much in return. Some fair comfort, perhaps.

— Think the province will be missing it?

— Dusty waited before answering, as though weighing a degree of honesty.

— I suppose they'll get another one. This one's half ruined, at least.

My security came from knowing that those I loved surrounded this quiet place. If I looked beyond, it was to gather.

— Where'd you take it from?
Again he paused. He jumped into the world yelling like he wanted everybody to know he'd arrived. Now year by year he'd grown gradually quieter.
— Killer Junction.
— Don't you think that's just asking for night terrors?

Dode, on the other hand, presented himself to the world as accompaniment. He sang with a voice that made the meadowlarks blush.

— I looked it over for blood if that's what you mean.
— That's no way for a Bible camp student to be speaking.
— Well, it's pretty cool though isn't it?

I once had a set of earrings, given by Avery to me on our 30th wedding anniversary. Both gave off goldish and silverish hues, not particularly shiny but certainly not drab. They consisted of two little orbs, one ended the pin, the other hung below on a tiny chain. I imagined that these reactionary moons followed the wanderings of my head.

Often after laying down to sleep I would push my back into the mattress and tuck my thumbs between my fingers.

Sometimes, once I began to drift, it felt as though my spine was being slowly pulled from a hole in the back of my neck. First there was a stretching of the skin as the cervical vertebrae were tugged. And then...pop. One vertebra popped out. Pop, another. Pop, pop.

Moon times. Lunar lit nights. There are matters that insist on a separate reasoning.

I will offer that one should enjoy the gritty aspects: bad haircuts, hangnails, scars, superficial scrapes, sunburns, scratchy throats, itchy ears, starchy shirts. Cherish the snit, the snide aside, the comeback.

Cherish most of all the hole in the shoe, because only through it can the topsoil be felt.

Perfection exists, truly and only in imperfection. Those who think they can lasso excellence have another thing coming, and that's called dissatisfaction.

The greatest beauty is found after denying reason. We cannot comprehend it or consider it, nor does it ask for consideration or comprehension. As soon as we reason, we recognize the situation from the ground up and we lose an empire of delicacy.

Only the dumb are obsessed with control.

Sandra and I had howdied but we hadn't shook. After church one Sunday Mama said she had something awfully important to do and for me to walk along with Sandy Paitre and her parents to the parking lot. Sandra and I lingered behind.

— The April Fools' dance is coming up at the Eagle Valley Community Hall, but I don't think I'm going.

— Me neither, you can bet on that. Only a dumb fool guy would go to a dance like that.

— Any girl'd be half a fool to accept an offer to go to a dance like that.

— Any guy'd be a fool for thinking any girl'd go with him even if he did ask.

— I wouldn't think of you as a fool.

— As long as you don't mind riding in the cab of a '47 three-quarter ton.

I didn't tell her I was paying off the $700 truck by working around the farm, which was pretty much the way I paid for everything.

Standing there giggling insanely with a bunch of her friends, all flowered out in the latest gewgaws of fashion, she kept looking at the box tied with an orange ribbon and acting as though I didn't know. I was surprised it was Sandra, not really surprised but it's just that I hadn't paid attention before. I think we took some chairs outside to the lawn and we ate the box lunch she had prepared but I don't remember what we talked about or much else of our time there.

I only remember that I spent time with her.

When we danced I held her up close. She smelled of warm cake icing mixed with roses.

We walked to the food table and I took a couple of those big chocolates and Sandra tugged at my sleeve.

— Maybe there's nothing you really want to eat right now.

She refused to even touch them.

— First time I ever heard of a girl not liking chocolates.

When I bit one my mouth filled with skunky juice and I rushed outside and spit the mess about as far as I could.

— Can't say I didn't warn you.

As odd as it sounds, that instant of spitting was also the moment I knew I wanted to ask for her hand. Took me a few more months to get up the nerve.

— All a steer can do is try.

And she accepted on the spot.

This spot. This spot of land where we sat and looked farther than I'd looked before.

Now that plot of tilled dirt is where I can say we planted our destiny.

When we were first married I used to joke the only ring I could afford was the beef ring.

We met Fridays over at Colburn & Sons. No deep freeze then, and sharing a cut cow was a good way to save some hard cash. But I think I went there as much for the news as for the beef.

— We brought forth sons and a daughter. See that barn?

I ran a thresher over this ground in the established tracks. I tested the soil with my elbow. I planted at full moon. I followed in the row of my father. When he passed on, the minister recalled his hardships. Times during the black blizzard when the entire land was blowing away; dirt piled so high they had to remove it from roads with snowplows; times when the sole bank foreclosed; times when soups were made from rawhide and bones. And yet he stayed. Hardly an obscenity from his lips either, through and through he was a God-fearing man with nothing but gentle words.

Worst I saw on the farm was the ice storm of '61, early July. Middle of the night Sandra kicking at my legs, a pounding like twenty marching bands up on the roof. Downstairs on the porch we saw slush slapping to the ground. Didn't have a garage so the car was getting all dinged up.

Three times the sky turned a tarnished silver. Shaft clouds were followed by ankle clouds and then by green clouds that forewarned the sort of storm that would pelt hail as large as a baby's fist. We had three storms that week and the second came down harder than slush, the third, ice balls the size of bulls' eyes. *Farmer's Almanac* didn't predict that one, said in fact it would be sunny and warm. The hail pulverized the alfalfa, first beating it down and then beating it up. It snapped limbs. It dented tin. It was a hail that could bash a man's brains.

Most people don't think about livestock in those situations, but hail that can shatter a car window or nick a tractor can easily kill. They say something like twenty thousand ducks died that day.

Afterwards I surveyed the havoc and I sat down and cried. It was once more than ruin, it was crop, it was food.

— I learned. Make a list. Title one Natural, title the other Unnatural.

I was forced to take a nine-month contract with a Japanese pipe company, office in Calgary. I travelled across the province making sure the pipes were delivered and numbered. Nearly a full year I ended up working there, writing up inventories on carbons held by a nickel-plated clip, counting product, making sure the shipments were delivered to the roughnecks.

I finally managed to put down on a PTO combine. Cut the cost by hitching it to the tractor rather than getting a self-propelled. Figured I'd leave that up to Dode on the day he took over.

One night a man showed up and tapped at the porch window. The first thing and last thing I remember about that man was his ragged boots. They'd ripped all the way along so I could see most of the length of his dirty feet. You'd have thought he stepped right out of those pictures of the Depression.

He said his car had busted down. Said they'd walked half way from Calgary. That's what he said, which I took to be a lie observing the state he was in and the fact there were many other houses between there and here. Sandra caught it first.

— Who's we?

The man looked like he was going to cry and he waved his hand into the darkness and a hollow-eyed woman appeared and then two girls about the same ages of our boys.

— Mister, I don't know who you are but there's always generosity in this house.

I knew about being out at the seat. I knew about general amnesty too. I'd seen immigrants helping out at haying time. I shoved back the door and the man bent to remove his busted boots and my boys dragged a couple chairs in from the parlour. Sandra presented what was left of our Sunday meal.

While a new pot of coffee brewed the man ate delicately. He'd wedge his fork underneath the hash and then he'd eye his girls and his wife. If they weren't eating he'd mumble something and they'd push food through their lips or if they were eating too fast he'd mumble something else and they'd push food around their plate. Then, apparently satisfied they were eating correctly he'd lift a tiny bit of the hash into his own mouth chewing as uneasily as I've ever seen anyone chew.

He told me in broken English that they'd fled Budapest when Soviet tanks and artillery had invaded, after the Hungarian uprising. He told me that over there he had been a first-class citizen.

As he talked of his trek across Canada, he slumped and pushed his eroded feet against the green and white Congoleum floor and he pressed his slow hands to the sides of his cup and he said: *Good luck hangs by a thread, bad luck by a thick rope.* And I could tell by his demeanour what he believed in.

God is always invoked by those who hold the big guns and by those who are defeated. But what about the rest? Surprise blizzards beat down high crops, banks rise and level the land, a chain unexpectedly breaks and an arm is maimed.

There is determination and there is accident.

How different to pick up the axe, pull the trigger, draw the whip. Slaughtering, massacring, butchering, these are the insane acts.

Their idea of goodness exacts killing. Their idea of goodness creates opportunities for ghastly acts.

We entered the Great War because it was the good and just action. We partook in the Second War as a war against evil. We interned the Japanese to Kananaskis and over there to Petawawa, Ontario. We forced Indians into reservations. We justified it all; we did all this for the good of our country. We're not alone in that. Two thousand years of war, more. How many millions dead. All done for the good of a country. When I pause to ponder just how much humanity's done for the good of a country since the dawn of civilization, I think it's a blessing we haven't done more good.

And here's another one to chew on. What about that John Love politician down there in Colorado, legalizing and supporting the smothering and cutting and sucking out of the product imagined by love. John Love. I spit on the name. John Love and free love and Vietnam. I spit on it all. John Hate. There's a better one.

And I spit on goodness too, at least the sort of goodness that intertwines with violence, that germinates hatred, denies concern, lacks compassion, snuffs lives. Yes, I spit on such goodness.

One year at the Grain Agricultural Society we hosted a Christmas party and Mr. White, who was Doctor here for many years, now retired, played Santa Claus for all the little ones. Dode got a tiny tractor and he carried it everywhere, saying that when he grew up he would have a real one just like it. It was never far from his sight, even when a front wheel broke off.

I want to fix it but there are some things no amount of doctoring will help.

When left alone, soil can starve so once every few years I planted a crop of sweet clover and when it started to bloom I'd plow it all under. I'm sure many a sightseer didn't have a clue about what I was doing when he looked out over the field. I'm sure he thought some idiot was plowing out his own grave.

There is accident. There is determination. There lies the difference.

I haven't talked about it and I won't talk about it, but after the accident, Sandra spent a lot of time at the church and reading her Book, the Good Book.

I noticed the chickadees, bobbing, flicking their heads, cracking and chucking sunflower shells from between their beaks. They skittishly jumped from feeder to mock orange. And right before, I paused to watch the little things.

The way I figure it, if you're human you have the obligation to be kind, and if you're not kind what does that make you?

On cold mornings I regularly went outside and added more seeds to the feeder.

Every season cannot be one of bumper crops. I think of the combine and of the columbine. I think of too many bean pots and an obituary for a tall man.

We drop handfuls of dirt because we must.

The most unnatural thing a man can do is dress Sunday best for his son's funeral.

People think of the prairie and they think of eye-filling expanses, mute clear skies, slow breathing clouds, forcing constant winds. The colours are pale opposites. Eventually a few tinged reds appear. They speak in low tones. Look closely: the occasional orchid, the stem of the dogwood, the wild rose. The brightest reds, the reds of a woman's lips and of wagons and of children's fire trucks, are not natural to the field. These are the reds of glossy Detroit paint and deep sanguine rivers. Two reds of objectionable hue.

I think of these things and I look upon the words as poetry. But out here words clot like curled leaves in the eaves.

Simple phrases are surpassed by the tingle of tin, the taught hum of barbed wire, a grass's massed miscellaneous susurruses, the bellow and brush of breezes.

Listen. Listen as I do, morning, noon, afternoon, a July or June. September.

Out here the undulating, unforgiving meadows are ruffled with more than one hundred varieties of grasses. The fields move as tides, forever tossed by the ebb and neap of air.

Now spring. A confetti of meadow crocuses ornaments the morning. A rising sun of flat broad hotness. Warmer breezes and the *cheerep* of robins. Notwithstanding, a tang of coolness requiring a cotton sweater. A mist across the fields and road. Wet grass from heavy dew. The new green of the living.

Ragged washboard roads that jar one's bones. Pity those who didn't visit the biffy first and had their teeth floating as the car bounded over those frost heaves.

Rubber tires on a gravel road make a sound in spring that is different than any other time of the year. The pebbles pop and skid from their chalky beds with a particular echo.

Even today I remember the fleeting flopping of my heart on those mornings.

The navy used to want prairie boys. Recruitment. They supplanted a woven ocean with one of brine and foam, weeds and sea—both billowy blown and cupped under a spread of sky. City boys, unable to coordinate bearings, might lose their sanity. Here too. Old bones bleached and brittle lay out here for ages. Like the sea the prairies don't offer much mercy.

Columbine grew. That anxious flowering carmine star returned every year. Avery rubbed it on the legs of our horses to increase their stamina. I once dug some from a Siffleur foothill field and planted the flowers around our flagpole. They remain.

Fly little flower, your dovetailed doves are red with passion, ring your rosies, drink from the well bowl and bow with shameful knowledge. Yours are the silky devil's tongs, one of a few hues competing with the solitary maple leaf. Spread your tiny alizarin flags, herald your cuckoldry.

There's fennel for you, and columbines: there's rue for you; and here's some for me... Proof my memory remains somewhat intact. Before that, well it was only fennel and anise and salt licorice: the tastes of youth.

Nothing Dusty wanted more than to have a car, almost since he was little even. He worked around here but spent a good deal of his free time, usually at night when I was kneading bread, balancing coins on the edge of his jar.

— '61 Chevy Impala two-door. I reason I don't need more than two doors.

He didn't say how much he paid for the used vehicle. He learned to drive it in the pasture, or more accurately around and around the pasture.

— Rocket red with metal siding and polished metal hubs. Get in you two.

He didn't have his license yet, but kids in this area had all been driving from about age thirteen. You had to on a farm. I figured with us on board he wouldn't try to smooth out the road. I took off my apron.

— Needs a bit of work, but not much.

— I don't think I ever sat in a car this fancy.

— Everything's red inside too. 'Cept the steering wheel. Half red and white.

He checked the mirror and his hair. He unhooked the straps of his overalls. He sat right up tall.

— And music. Everything you might want in an automobile.

He turned on the radio and it played some twangy country ballad that I didn't know but Dusty hummed along. He shifted into drive and we looped the yard and we drove for a while up 27. He blew the horn at some horses that might have cared less and after we'd gone a while longer I said I needed to get back, Sheryn-Lee hadn't eaten lunch. And like a gentleman he immediately swung around and headed back home.

— You got a nice fine thing here.

— Yeah. I do.

Avery never approved.

— Big waste of money. Better to train a fire hose on boys who think they need that much freedom.

— Boy needs a car these days. It's not like it was when everyone just stayed around home.

One afternoon when the magpies were hassling a tabby cat around the yard, Dusty drove me and Sheryn-Lee all the way to the Olds Co-op. The first thing we saw was the grain elevator, same as we'd seen a hundred times, with the name of the company in big letters and OLDS painted below in smaller letters. I told them what I always said about prairie towns.

— Find the grain elevator and you've located Main Street.

We returned at dusk and called out padiddle and touched the roof whenever we spotted a car with only one torch.

— You know what I sometimes think? I think Canada is a great sleeping bairn, and the prairies are his acres of parted hair before the wrinkled brow of the Rockies.

I baked two pies for fall supper, Saskatoon berry and sweet-squash. Nothing as nice as a clean meal, and if you're on the cooking committee the dishes can wait, but we pitched in anyway, all us women and one man. That was Reverend Johnson who always did the largest part of the scrubbing.

— I'll clean them right down to their souls.

— Just so long as you don't scrub off the name tape.

Legs flew past the basement window as younger children played run-and-chase outside on the lawn.

Everybody laughed over Mabel's pie. She didn't soak the figs before baking it; they called it shoe-leather pie.

— Where's your brother's guitar?

— No idea.

— Your Papa ask you to bring it?

Dusty pressed his lips to a thin line.

— I guess.

— So I guess you now got to go right back and get it. And this isn't coming from your Papa this is coming from me.

— I don't see anyone rushing 'round to pick up my things when I need them.

I suppose he didn't know Avery was behind him until his ear was half yanked off.

Took Dode with him.

— Got to talk some sense into that damn fool boy.

— He'll grow.

— Cut a couple slabs of pie. They'll be back before we finish the crust and *Sally Goodin'* will be bustin' the rafters.

I never liked the fact that *eventually* is too often another word for *finally*.

When the rain came it was all drizzle. And when the boys didn't show we made our goodbyes and we took our car and we drove the wet route toward home.

About three miles down we saw where Dusty's car had flipped into the berm. Avery slowed. He stopped the car. Left the wipers running. We ran across the road to Dusty who lay all humped up, grimacing in the grass, evidently tossed from the car, scraped, alive, knocked half loopy, alive, a couple cuts, alive and alive.

Dode.

Dode lay, sideways, half against the dashboard.

The blushings of his once cheery cheeks had leaked all out and run down his arm. An unlovable puddle.

A car pulled up. I sat on the edge of the road cradling Dusty in my arms. I don't know why I sat on the edge of the road in the wet and in the mud rather than in my own car. At least Sheryn-Lee stayed in the back seat. A door slammed and I held Dusty and I stared out over the badger brush into the field at a group of dark mottled cattle that stood braced against the spit.

I remembered the times, Saturday mornings, when the two boys and I used to march and sing along to Porky Charbonneau's show. I thought about how the amount of rain determines how tall the grasses will be. When Dode was little he used to prance around singing *Sixteen Chickens and a Tambourine.* He used to stand in the rain for hours.

— Life's hardships should make one better, not bitter.
— Nobody agrees with that.

My least favourite days are these drizzly ones. At these times the fog settles onto the land and mist turns the trees to rawboned besoms. Grasses ache with monotony. Fields sag and dampen. They lose their willy-nilly spirit. When the mist takes over we lack the indication of the fences, but even so.

— These days close me in.
— Days passed. Days pass. Think of time as a comforter on a bed.

Back east the autumn mountains glow like searing embers. Out here, amidst the browns, reds are the most unnatural.

To understand the colours of these flat lands one must understand the oranges and the blues, complementaries on a wheel of paint, brightly touting each other's difference, unstapled to any holiday.

How camouflaged the western bluebird is out here, belly a sand-worn orange of the land, back a mirror reflection of the sky. This little bird is an earth and heaven all its own.

The foothills demonstrate oranges that are less than orange.

Out here we have the deaf oranges, radiant only when raked by morning or sunset light. These less-than-oranges dye bales of hay ocher and fling sand upon deer hides. The less-than-oranges tinge twig and tree, they burn upon wire and fence and road.

They tan a face.

And above all this: no blue exists as sharp and tiffany as that of the winter Alberta sky. Even in the summer it appears as a chilly veil simultaneously distant and sitting on the surface of the eye.

On a hot day the blue fades all distant objects. On a patchwork afternoon the blue turns to the wash of a river stone.

The blue of evening tousles all beneath its hand: fence poles, foreheads, backs of birds, shadows of bulls, treads of tractors, sallow larches.

As the sun drops and the day grows colder, the transparent sky flows like watercolour from orange to blue. The colours lessen.

The day lengthens, farthest points stop begging.

In the distance the blues shift.
In the distance the blues sift.
And they soften.
And they smudge.
And they blur.

And the thud?

The horizon.

October 9, 1971, that was a Saturday. Some markers you never forget. We were at fall supper at Sundre United. They had a big basement painted in battleship grey. Whoever wanted to be a part of the meal would bring out a dish and we'd set up the long tables and everybody would take some of what they wanted, of course there were too many pots of baked beans and a fair number of pies. The church would get the coffee going and some of the children would get together and put on a harvest play for our entertainment and then a few of the older boys would get out the fiddles and banjos and guitars.

Dode was the one who was always outside. I'd yell, pitch a hand, and he'd throw a flake of hay as if his clock needed winding. Sometimes he'd disappear and someone would have seen him over at Stockwell's thumbing through a magazine or they'd spy him with his stuff out in a copse smoking kinnikinnick or *Old Chum, The Tobacco of Quality.*

— That kid couldn't walk by a cemetery without relieving himself on a grave. Damn irreverent fool.
— You don't go around speaking poorly…
— Just in a phase.

I usually had the last word in conversations like this one although I knew Sandra's silence was more of a word than my own. Even so, I pretty much knew, from my own experience, what was going on in a boy's head, and better yet what a boy was made of.

And his brother, standing near a pole, eyeing the girls, maybe thinking he could mole his way out of his duty. And when he started back talking I'd seen enough.

— Why were you arguing with your mother?

— I wasn't.

— You want a kicking?

He shrugged and gave a sweet smile to his mother and walked out of the basement, got in his car with Dode, slammed the door, and gunned it out of the parking lot.

— Close the gate! Heaven help you if you don't hear.

I think about the columbine and the combine. I think about my life.

Where reverence walks, hands hold naiveté.

It was early in the evening. October. Avery said he'd take a smoke in the barn but I never saw a light. Nothing. No spark anywhere in the back forty beyond that stable door.

I rocked. The air was cool. No moon, the needlepoint lay on the little table next to me. I pulled my sweater sleeves over my fingertips.

— Cold hands, warm heart. Dirty feet, no sweetheart.

A clomping on the step, a clearing of a throat and a pause by a man who gave three solid knocks on the wooden railing even though he stood just before me. I'd never seen him. He took a large flashlight from his pocket and turned it on and shined it up onto his face and I noticed a spot of blood marked the side of his clean shaven jaw. He smiled with a smile that showed no teeth. Even a tramp will show the few teeth he has.

— Beg your pardon, ma'am. May I take a moment of your time tonight?

I knew Avery was in the barn even though it remained dark.

— Little late to be out, isn't it?

— Thank you ma'am.

The visitor sat heavily on the stoop and turned his flashlight off.

— Mister would you like a cup of coffee? I pride myself on being hospitable. It may be watered down but it's hot.

— Not if it's trouble. If it's no trouble then what I say is there's always fellowship where there's a pot of coffee. And if it's no trouble I say I don't mind if I do.

I went to get it. He rose and followed me inside. I thought I should give a holler over to Avery but I let it rest. I poured a cup and slid the sugar.

— No bother ma'am.

I took another cup down from the shelf while he gulped at his coffee.

I knew Dusty was upstairs in what used to be his shared bedroom lying on his bed underneath a few pictures of Wayne the Thumper Harris, lineman for the Stampeders, and looking at that big stop sign with the bullet holes in it, and I knew Sheryn-Lee was in the parlour listening to the radio, and I knew Avery was in the barn, and I knew Dode was over at Mountain View Cemetery lying with his eyes stitched tight.

— Ma'am, I'm here to share good news.

There could be tears in cups of coffee but not in front of this man.

— That news is that whosoever believeth in him should not perish, but have eternal life.

On many twilit evenings Sandra would sit and finger tunes from her book of favourite songs. I remember "Camptown Races" and "Clementine," songs everybody knew. I'd take my craving outside on the porch with my feet propped against the railing and I'd listen to her play and I'd exhale toward Venus.

Until I merged into the streaming flow, until I became what I became; I have since moved from specific moment to collective memory.

— I go out the door I entered.
— Not in life you don't.

Avery's song

I think of the passing; of past and peace.
A candle is seen a long way on grasslands:
      o'er arching of worldly form and distance.
The migrating hawk flees:
      the oiled road and grey sage are beclouded with the same ease.
Oh, although dull and tongue-tied the shadow touches us all,
      wants to end all longing: wants to offer up;
      a cope of lucent and unscarred sky.
The elevator with Jesus scripture was torn down before I knew absence.
      You described wire like a frill
      crisscrossing the townships,
Finery upon a landscape that needed none but the face you wore:
      And now following your lead I will shift and dispense.

Sandra's song

The sky is my passage; it moves with me.
Darkenings, brightenings, an expansiveness:
　　　it urges me toward the unbreakable.
It reinstates my hope:
　　　requests innocence and offers a bell-clack of certainty.
Oh, though I rove on through dateless day and night-times of time,
　　　I will keep this foremost: that you were my soul;
　　　my sun and my single constant breath.
You constructed a double rainbow as a means of comfort in that moment:
　　　you guided my eyes past black soil;
　　　over rough rain torn fencecaps.
Clarity is born not of reprieve but compensation, allow this:
　　　and we will know a mile up and a mile advancing.

The earliest missionary to step out here was George McDougall. He thought this land rich and he confessed the mountains enough for a view.

They say the name of our town is an Indian word meaning little village. Or it was a Norwegian word, from *sondre* meaning south. I tend toward the latter meaning, being we sit at the south end of a tornado alley that runs clear up to Edmonton. They opened the post office here in 1909. Settled on the name the same year. Even so, the place wasn't designated a town until forty-seven years later.

I think back on my boys who, as teenagers, used to take traps out into the fields to catch pocket gophers. They'd each set their trap into a hole and they'd wait. It was rare they'd find one early in the day but after supper one trap would usually have one. The boys took a broken axe handle and hit the animals on the head until blood came out their ears and eyes and noses. Then they'd bring their traps inside to scald away the scent of blood and they'd write the date and the number they'd caught on the list taped to the wall in the kitchen so I'd know how many dimes to hand them.

One week they trapped more than sixty gophers. Other times the boys would put water down the gopher holes to make sure they were empty before filling them with dirt. They knew a horse would snap a leg if it stepped into one of them.

They framed their actions.

This need, this need to frame actions, must be some justification resulting from human nature. I never much saw the hare or coyote worrying about its actions. I never saw the bee contemplate the taking of pollen from a flower, or the bird trouble itself about the worm held in its beak.

I'm not trying to determine what is good. I know what is good. Sandra was pure enough, if I can speak in the past.

I know evil just as clearly. I've heard of a minister who, after sitting in the sacred house of the almighty for more months than I ever did, deflowered a girl of hardly twelve. I've seen men, on the TV news, who butchered a hundred townspeople in one day and who then bent down to pass the bloodied knife to their children.

Once I thought of simple things, like hailstones.
Now I wish I could think of simple things.

Once it all seemed so simple, with Sandra too, and then she couldn't even swallow.

She never spoke of it aloud. Never the word. She acted as though she didn't know; she knew. You don't have something eating you from womb to woman without knowing more than you want to know.

I think of the suspended footbridge where I first took Sandra's picture. It was a thin instant over an eternally running river. We stood together on that old wooden structure. It's all metal now. When they replaced it in 1958, Dode would have been six, Dusty four. Sheryn-Lee wasn't even a speck. She'd come later, always my little girl, forever tippy-toed, straining and rushing to edges.

In 1915 the flood came through Sundre. I learned this from my father who saw the town bridge and ferry wiped out.

Another bridge replaced. All I know is the neat and strong concrete, well lit by streetlights on a straight sidewalk.

February 7, 1962, as clear as the hoof I've shod a hundred times. Temperature rose from -2 to 71 degrees in an hour. Now you tell me about weather. I woke up wearing a winter coat and went to bed with swimming trunks.

I don't know why I remember such things, just learned them once or twice and they stuck. Clothes make the man I guess.

— Dode moved on.
— We shift about for a time before we shift along.

The farm was meant to go to Dusty, but he went his own way too. Each of us must till for the future.

— I built an empire of dust.
— You have done enough. There is no fault.

At first she felt the sting. Later came the blood. I won't talk about her suffering. It's not that I can't. I won't. No reason to give it more than it was.

In '65 you could get two good weaning cows for a hundred-twenty-five dollars and it was said to constitute a good deal.
I always found that routine and course were the temporary pacifiers. The future roared up soon enough, reversing the day in slow motion, allowing the skies to leak, cleaving, hewing, disembowelling all pattern.

Today I look across at the place where we held each other around the waist for the first time. I look farther and it's grasslands straight to Texas.

The iron rusts. The petal wilts. The board cracks. The axe of God.

— Don't assign fault.

Most of all I considered mercy. Such things should not be planned but she was shifting. I won't couch, she was suffering. I built a barn, dammit, a shed. More. I know post and beam, rafters, girts, purlins. I know joints and connections. I know a strong frame. And yet I know nothing. The doctors knew less.

She couldn't swallow. What are a man's hands to do with that?

When the sun hangs low we rotate the hands of clocks back an hour. We attempt to balance the irregularity and arbitrariness of our lives against the tilt of the earth.

Awake. I located the slant of Orion the Hunter, the last of the winter constellations, and I followed its three stars as they silently slid west across the framed heavens. The bolder stars of the Crux appeared through the window, their brightnesses rising and falling with the wind. And then I watched the sky fold from hat dark to velvet blue and I believed I could hear notes of music.

I ran my finger along the wavy edge of the picture I'd once snapped of her. She'd tucked it into the frame of the mirror over her dresser but I'd taken to carrying it in the front pocket of my shirt.

I knew she'd gone outside to sit on the porch as she did nearly every morning, as cold as it was. Her one desire was to breathe in. She desired to fill her lungs more than her body would allow, maybe. She'd expand her chest with burning cold air, just to feel it. A hunger maybe. A divine torture.

A house divided is a splayed pack of cards. She wanted her home intact.

She read more than anyone I knew. She'd read bunches of books, poetry, the newspaper. She recalled, if not exact details, the foundations of arguments. She was convincing, and she could see what was fair and just, what was already a remembrance and how it should be. My opinion counted but a time comes when thinking cannot answer for need.

Action and action.

A repeating hope, maybe. Even then I knew I would stay with her. Sometimes foresight is stronger than hindsight, 0-0, double-aught.

I set the cardboard box onto the edge of the dresser. I wondered whether last thoughts mattered. I wanted my own last thought to be full of love and remembrance.

The morning shine made gold a strand of her long grey hair that had been trapped by a sliver of wood on her jewelry box. Beside it stood a bottle of pale perfume with a bright cap. Her gold clock appeared to be ticking but I heard no sound. A tiny figurine of a bird sat atop a white tatted doily. A cornflower blue book printed *Longfellow* in gold was aligned parallel to the edges of the dresser. Nearby rested her wire-framed reading glasses and her kid-skin cyclamen purse. A vase held the pussy willows I'd driven all the way to Olds to get for her.

I smelled the crackling heat of the sun, and I smelled the musty heat of the furnace.

All I remember.

All I wish to remember is how those little sparrows fled as
fast as a spark, a drumming flutter past the bush. That's what I
remember. All,

all I wanted to see, all I didn't want to see.

Recollection is such a thin and delicate fibre, as if we see through the wobbling heat from a burning-barrel.

Avery and I never trespassed on each other's ground. I don't know that we despoiled the earth either. We only borrowed the land, never with malice, simply with propriety.

One Christmas we drove the boys into Calgary and we all rode up to the top of the Husky Tower. Sixty-three seconds to the entire view. Afterwards we ate dinner at a Chinese café where Avery asked for a potato because he never enjoyed eating rice. Before driving back he kicked off the icy snard-lumps that had formed behind the wheels. By the time we got home, both boys were throwing up because of some flu they'd gotten at school perhaps. I knew because of their temperatures.

You can plant columbine out here any time of the year, they call it crow's foot and granny's bonnet. It's fairly long lived. What though, do we plant that remembers us?

The solemn season is always predicted by the movement of the clouds. At that time the sun sets to dusky dim, and the evening settles over the blessed, and over the solitary, over the combine and the columbine.

Eventually the once declared is whispered, even as the wind gets on all fours.

Everything passes. That which we deemed our terrible secret, passes. That which we celebrated as our singing joy, it too passes.

I gave the boys Alpenkräuter, stomach bitters to reduce their nausea.

Ultimately, there isn't good, or there isn't evil. There are occurrences. Perhaps it is the memories that mean the most.

Before we had a dryer I always hung the white sheets outside, spring, summer, winter, it didn't matter. I held the clothespins in my mouth and reached up to the line with two hands. I recall sheets made diaphanous by the late sun, and around me honeybees, flowers finally finding peace, bats flapping out routes in blindness. Once when it was below zero Dode hucked a snowball clear through one of the sheets and the sky tumbled in.

I am most sure of my memory.

Once I hung my heart on a tree limb and forced nature down the gullet. Now I expect a time when breezes no longer flow with names and even memory's moon no longer wanes and waxes. I expect a time not so long forward when pink new fingers trace over grey photographs.

Only the foolhardy waste time on consideration. Avery was a namer. He acquired names for all sorts of things. Fry you up a pan of prairie fish? He'd ask me while swinging a slab of bone white tripe over the sink. Or he'd tell the children they might have as many bull fries as they wanted, meaning, well, a part of the bull. Funny how some names remain and some fade. And he'd say the prairie grace:
— God bless the skin and bone. To hell with the meat and damn the bone.

People want to ask what is out here, what do we see. Do we see what we choose to see?

I think what I miss most are Avery's cracked weather-beaten fingers and how his shoulders darkened and hardened. How the hair across his chest became whiter and softer as he aged.

Not much to touch out here. Not anymore. Not that way.

We don't master death by attending funerals. We don't learn to deal with death by glancing in a sideways sort of way at other people's deaths.

I considered. A season is long enough. Sometimes the Indian summer extends the warmth. Then come the nights when the prairie undulates in darkness, a heavy wash, rolls of thick expanse. Out here silence is never as silent as you think it will be.

So the question won't linger, I decided what I wanted. I asked him plain, in so many words.

My memories are my weight. I have often wondered which picture memory I remember more, the face of my son at birth or at death.

In both instances I have wanted to cover him with a comforter because I was afraid of the cold for him.

I recall as a little girl reading of a whole town that up and moved. Houses, hotels, businesses, all gone, things just left, dishes, furniture, things too expensive to take. I recall pressing a tab on the back of the *Quik* margarine bag and kneading for twenty minutes to make it yellow. I remember seeing *Four Faces West* at the Chinook Park Drive-In. I received pussy willows from Avery that signalled spring and I placed them in a blue vase.

I never was an especially tall woman. There are many places I was unable to reach. But I was jolly. I used to dangle my feet. What a phrase now.

There was.

There was the most absolutely singular quality of light that morning. And on that very morning one little thing landed on my arm! First time, and it hooked little claws upon the stitched blanket. A glint on its tiny talon, shiny black. One deep sable eye questioning, a movement of clarity, an exactness before the flight.

I cupped in my outstretched hand the love of only you and I brought it close to my buttons. In the other palm I balanced the love of my children.

And I know that what we were can no longer be. And I know that what we are cannot be said.

Everywhere and neverwhere, everyway and neverway, everything and neverthing,

beyond and beyondness.

ESPLANADE
Books

THE FICTION SERIES AT VÉHICULE PRESS

[Andrew Steinmetz, editor]

A House by the Sea : A novel by Sikeena Karmali

A Short Journey by Car : Stories by Liam Durcan

Seventeen Tomatoes : *Tales from Kashmir* : Stories by Jaspreet Singh

Garbage Head : A novel by Christopher Willard

The Rent Collector : A novel by B. Glen Rotchin

Dead Man's Float : A novel by Nicholas Maes

Optique : Stories by Clayton Bailey

Out of Cleveland : Stories by Lolette Kuby

Pardon Our Monsters : Stories by Andrew Hood

Chef : A novel by Jaspreet Singh

Orfeo : A novel by Hans-Jürgen Greif

Anna's Shadow : A novel by David Manicom

Sundre : A novel by Christopher Willard

Véhicule Press
www.vehiculepress.com